*Dec. 15, 2002*

*To Julia,*

*Love from*

*Thelma.*

ROBIN

These stories are all true,
they are for all those of you
who have never had the opportunity
to get to know chickens.

Text Copyright © 1998 Pamela Adams
Illustrations Copyright © 1998 Robin Currie
Layout and typesetting by Uri Cogan
Printed in Canada by
Morriss Printing Company Ltd.
All Rights Reserved
For information about permission
to reproduce selections from this book,
or to re-order, contact Pam Adams
Box 497 Ganges P.O.
Salt Spring Island  BC  V8K 2W1  Canada
ISBN 0-9684415-0-5

First Printing November 1998
Second Printing April 1999

# BLOSSOM AND FRIENDS

by Pamela Adams
illustrated by Robin Currie

A SALT SPRING PUBLISHING COMPANY

Thank you
to Joe for his patience,
and to Robin for giving
so much of his precious time.

At the end
of the garden,
there is a little house,
with a red roof and a small green door.
This is where the chickens live.
They all have names and you will
meet some of them in these stories.

Early each morning,
the lady walks down the garden,
to the little house and opens
the small green door.
Whenever the door is opened,
it is never early enough for the chickens.
They always
run out
very fast.

Little Brave One
is always first
out of the chicken house.
She is a fearless and brave explorer.
As chickens are not toilet trained,
they are never allowed in the house
where the people live.
The lady is always very careful
to close the door.

One day the door was left

open!

and so,
being a fearless and brave explorer,
in
walked
Little Brave One.

There on the floor,
waiting to be tasted,
was a bowl of cat food.
Little Brave One discovered
that chickens love cat food.

That night
in the chicken house,
all the others listened
in amazement,
as Little Brave One
told of her daring dash into the house,
and of the delicious cat food.
When she had finished her story,
no-one spoke for a long time.
Finally Blossom said "Grock, grock, grock,"
and it was time to go to sleep.

Like the door
to the house,

the gate to
the vegetable garden
was always closed.
NO CHICKENS ALLOWED.
The chickens didn't understand this rule.
They had seen the lady digging,
and knew they were very good at digging.
They had strong legs and could
dig up a plant in no time at all.
They were especially good at finding
the bugs that live in the roots of plants.

So it was a real surprise
when Funny Snail found the gate
open!

She called to the others…
and in
they all
went.

The soil was easy
to dig and

there were lots of
worms and grubs.

There were bugs

of all shapes

and sizes.

14

What a wonderful garden party they had,
until the lady noticed

that the gate was open!

That night
in the chicken house,
they all talked happily
of the wonderful things
they had found to eat
in the garden.
"Grock, grock, grock" said Blossom
and it was time to go to sleep.

At the end
of the garden,
in the little house,
the chickens were shouting.
It was time for the lady to let them out.
She just didn't understand,
how important it was
to be let out this morning.

It had rained all night
　　　and there would be

　　　　　　　　　　worms
　　　　　　　　　　　　everywhere.

By the time the people, in their house,
were having breakfast,
the chickens were so full,
they couldn't have eaten another worm,
even if it had wriggled right over
　　　　　　　　　　　their
　　　　　　　　　　toes.

They sat under the guest cabin,
and preened their feathers.
It takes a long time to keep feathers
in good condition.

Blossom
was the last one to leave.
She was always last to do anything.

As she walked past the house,

Blossom noticed
that the door
had been left open again.
She went in very carefully.
straight to the kitchen,
but the cat bowl was empty.

At the other end of the house,
there was a little girl in bed,
watching television.
It looked like fun,
so Blossom flew up
onto a chair
and watched as well.
She had a great time
until
the lady came back
into
     the
          house……

That night
in the chicken house,
all the others listened
in amazement as Blossom
told of the wonders of television.
When she had finished,
no-one spoke for a long time.
At last Blossom said "Grock, grock, grock,"
and it was time to go to sleep.

In the little house,
at the end of the garden,
there were a lot of excited chickens.
The first egg had been laid.
It was a lovely dark brown one.
Everyone was very impressed.
The chicken who had laid it
jumped out of the nest,
so that the others could admire her egg.

She shouted
as loud as she could,
"Egg, egg, egg."
Today she had become
a very important chicken.
The little girl named the chicken, "Egg",
so that all would remember this day.

Egg was especially careful
to eat lots of good food that day.
She wanted to lay another egg
as beautiful as the first.
She ate a lot of clover,

she ate a worm,

she ate a bug,

ROBIN

she ate some grain.

Then she found,
hiding in the rocks......

...... a snake!

Egg picked it up and disappeared quietly
into the cover of some bushes.
She knew if the others saw the snake,
they would chase her and make her share.
They did see,
      and chased her,
           and made her share.

That night
in the chicken house,
Egg told the others
all about laying eggs.
The chickens listened carefully,
for they knew that one day soon,
they too, would lay eggs.
"Grock" said Blossom,
"Grock, grock, grock,"
and it was time to go to sleep.

Upon the little house,
at the end of the garden,
snow had been falling all night.
The lady had dug a path,
all the way from her house,
to the chicken house.
When she opened the green door,
Comby peeked out and wondered
where all the grass and clover had gone.

Later that day,
the chickens were
getting restless.
So little Brave One
led an expedition.
They went down the path the lady had dug.
The chickens had to stretch very tall,
to see over the sides of the path.
All they could see was white everywhere.
It was very scary.

The people had laughed and played
in the snow all morning.
The chickens were curious.
What could there be
on a day like this
that was so much fun?

It was Comby,
who found
the strange snow creature,
with the grain scattered at its feet.

That night
in the chicken house,
the chickens decided
that they didn't like snow.
There was no clover, no grass,
and it was hard to find bugs.
The mice and snakes seemed to have
vanished.
"Grock, grock," said Blossom.
"Grock, grock, grock,"
and it was time to go to sleep.

Who knows what new adventures
the chickens will have
when the snow melts?